Sir Laugh-A-Lot

By Katie Dale

Illustrated by Jon Davis

Chapter 1

Lancelot's dad was a knight. Lancelot's grandad had been a knight too. And Lancelot's great-grandad had been a knight as well. In fact, ALL the men in Lancelot's family had been knights, for as long as anyone could remember.

So when Lancelot was born, his family was very excited.

“It’s a boy!” his dad cried. “We’ll call him Lancelot, after the most famous knight of all!”

“That’s a good name,” his grandad agreed, smiling.

“A good, strong name,” his great-grandad agreed, grinning.

“A good, strong, knightly name!” his dad cried. “Lancelot will be a good, strong knight!”

Everyone beamed... except Lancelot, who giggled.

Lancelot couldn’t wait to go to Knight School to learn to be a proper knight! But all the other boys were brave and strong. Lancelot was neither.

“Look out, Lancelot!” the jousting teacher cried, as Lancelot tripped over his lance.

The other boys laughed.

“Look out, Lancelot!” the combat teacher cried, when Lancelot’s helmet fell shut and he crashed into everything. The other boys laughed.

“Look out, Lancelot!” his riding teacher cried, as Lancelot fell off his horse into a big pile of manure. The other boys laughed. Poor Lancelot wasn’t good at anything - except making people laugh!

Lancelot sighed... then he smiled... then he laughed! Because he’d finally found something he was good at!

Every day, Lancelot made the other boys laugh by clowning around, joking and pulling funny faces. He soon became the most popular boy at Knight School!

Chapter 2

Then one day, Lancelot's dad had some exciting news.

"The king's holding a royal tournament!" he cried, slapping Lancelot on the back so hard he nearly fell over.

"Anyone in the land can compete," his grandad added excitedly, shaking Lancelot so hard his teeth rattled.

"And the winner will become Princess Rosalie's personal knight and live in the castle!" his great-grandad exclaimed, waving his stick around so much Lancelot nearly tripped over it.

"Just imagine if you won, Lancelot!" his dad said. "We'd all be so proud!"

"So very proud!" added his grandad.

"So very VERY proud!" added his great-grandad. "None of the knights in our whole family have ever lived in the castle!"

They all beamed at Lancelot, hope shining in their eyes.

Lancelot swallowed hard. "I'll... I'll do my b-best!" he stammered.

Poor Lancelot trained harder than ever. More than anything, he wanted to make his family proud.

He trained morning, noon, and night...

But it was no good.

"Sleep well, Lancelot!" his dad said.

"Sweet dreams!" his grandad called.

"Good night!" his great-grandad yelled.

Poor Lancelot slumped onto the floor. "I'll never be a good knight," he sighed sadly.

Finally the day of the tournament arrived.

Knights from all over the land came to compete. Knights in gold armour, silver armour, and even a knight in shining red armour. They all paraded around the crowded arena before the tournament.

Lancelot gulped. He had never seen so many people! This was going to be so embarrassing. Worse still, there, in the front row, were Lancelot's dad, grandad, and great-grandad.

Suddenly a trumpet fanfare played, and the king arrived.

"Greetings, my loyal subjects!" the king cried. "Welcome to the Royal Tournament. I look forward to a day of bravery, skill, and strength! And most of all, I look forward to welcoming the winning knight to my castle, to guard my most precious treasure, Princess Rosalie."

Everyone cheered. Another trumpet fanfare played, and the tournament began!

Chapter 3

The knights took turns to joust in pairs.

First to compete were the Red Knight and the enormous Silver Knight.

"Ready, steady, GO!" cried the king.

The ground trembled as the horses galloped towards each other.

BASH! The knights' lances hit each other's shields noisily.

CRASH! The Silver Knight tumbled off his horse, onto the ground.

The crowd cheered as the Silver Knight slumped away, and the Red Knight celebrated.

Lancelot gulped. The Silver Knight was twice as big as the Red Knight! If he was so easily beaten, Lancelot didn't stand a chance.

But soon it seemed that no one stood a chance against the Red Knight.

One by one, he beat every other knight in the tournament.

BASH! CRASH!
BASH! CRASH!
BASH! BASH! CRASH!

Finally, it was Lancelot's turn.

"Go, Lancelot!" his dad cried.

"You can do it!" his grandad called.

"We're so proud of you!" his great-grandad yelled.

Lancelot gulped. They wouldn't be proud of him for long.

"Ready, steady, GO!" cried the king.

The Red Knight's horse galloped towards Lancelot. Lancelot trembled so much his armour rattled.

"Come on, Lancelot!" his dad shouted.

“What are you waiting for?” his grandad cried.

“Go get him!” his great-grandad yelled.

Lancelot swallowed hard. More than anything, he just wanted to turn and run away as fast as he could... but he’d promised his family that he’d try his best.

“C-come on, horsey!” Lancelot stammered, nudging his horse. “We’ve got to try!”

Lancelot’s horse broke into a slow trot, and then a canter, and finally a gallop. Lancelot held on tight, praying he wouldn’t fall off his horse, drop his lance, or embarrass his family too much!

The Red Knight galloped closer and closer, his armour glinting in the sunlight, his pointy lance aimed right at Lancelot's chest!

Lancelot gulped, and closed his eyes tight... then suddenly, he had an idea!

Chapter 4

At the last minute, just as the Red Knight lunged for him, Lancelot leaned far back in his saddle – and the Red Knight's lance missed him!

Everyone gasped.

The Red Knight looked round, surprised. As they both turned round to gallop towards each other again, Lancelot thought quickly.

He couldn't use the same trick twice...

"Sorry about that!" Lancelot called, as the Red Knight aimed his lance at him again. "I was feeling a bit tired. I've been working the **knight shift**. Get it?"

The Red Knight chuckled and his lance jiggled so much he missed Lancelot again!

Everyone gasped.

Lancelot smiled.

The next time the Red Knight charged towards him, Lancelot took his helmet and shield off, pulled lots of funny faces and waggled his eyebrows.

The Red Knight laughed so much, he stopped galloping, and his horse slowed to stop by Lancelot's side.

"I've never fought anyone like you!" the Red Knight laughed. "What kind of knight are you?"

"A wimpy one," Lancelot grinned. "I'm **Sir Render** - get it?" The Red Knight laughed so hard he fell off his horse!

Lancelot grinned. "Does that mean I win and become Princess Rosalie's personal guard and live in the castle?"

"Not exactly," the Red Knight chuckled, taking off his helmet.

Everyone gasped...

Chapter 5

The Red Knight was Princess Rosalie! The crowd went silent, the king's jaw dropped, and Lancelot's cheeks turned as red as Princess Rosalie's armour.

“I’ve beaten every knight in the land,” Princess Rosalie grinned. “So I don’t think I need a guard, do you, Father?”

The king laughed and shook his head. “No, I don’t think you do,” he chuckled.

“But it’s ages since anyone made me laugh as much as you,” Princess Rosalie smiled at Lancelot. “Will you come and live in the castle, and be my royal entertainer?”

Lancelot grinned. “I’d love to!”

“Wonderful!” Princess Rosalie grinned. “Kneel please.”

Lancelot jumped off his horse and Princess Rosalie tapped him lightly on each shoulder with her sword.

"I now proclaim you Sir Laugh-A-Lot – the royal entertainer!" she cried.

Everyone cheered.

"We're so proud of you!" his dad cried.

"So very proud!" his grandad called.

"So very, very proud indeed!" his great-grandad yelled, grinning. "But then, we always have been, and we always will be!"

Lancelot beamed.

"Hooray for Sir Laugh-A-Lot!" everyone cried happily.

The End

Pink
Red
Yellow
Blue
Green
Orange
Turquoise
Purple
Gold
White

Book Bands for Guided Reading

The Institute of Education book banding system is a scale of colours that reflects the various levels of reading difficulty. The bands are assigned by taking into account the content, the language style, the layout and phonics. Word, phrase and sentence level work is also taken into consideration.

Maverick Early Readers are a bright, attractive range of books covering the pink to white bands. All of these books have been book banded for guided reading to the industry standard and edited by a leading educational consultant.

To view the whole Maverick Readers scheme, visit our website at www.maverickearlyreaders.com

Or scan the QR code above to view our scheme instantly!